LITTLE VAMPIRE

Stories and Drawings by

Joann Sfar

Colors by Walter
Translated by Alexis Siegel
and Edward Gauvin

First Second
New York & London

Table of Contents

"Little Vampire Goes to School"

It was a night just like any other night at the old mansion.
The dead stepped out, dressed in their Sunday best.
Where are you going this evening, my dear?
To play bridge.
Would you give me your daughter's hand?
We lost it.
Still got her foot if ya want.
Teapots danced with tables, and ghosts kept time with their chains.

Ancestors slipped out of their dusty portraits to have a little fun as they did every night. All was well, and yet somebody was sad.
Hey! That's my wife!
I want to go to school.
No Little Vampire had ever asked such a thing. The ghosts were aghast.
Vampires are free as the wind. They can fly; they can turn themselves into rats, wolves, or bats; they can even bite little girls till they bleed, without ever getting into trouble with their parents.
So really, Little Vampire...
Don't you have something better to do than go to school?
No.

I'm bored here. There aren't any other children around.

But you have Phantomato, your dog.
Yeah!

I know, but he's a dog. I want to see kids my own age.
Hmf!

Everyone found Little Vampire's request very strange, especially his dog, who was a bit hurt that Little Vampire would prefer kids his own age over him.

And what's that supposed to mean, anyway-"his own age"?

A vampire doesn't have an "age".

As soon as he became a vampire, he stopped growing old, so what's all this nonsense?

Don't be mean, Phantomato. You can see this school thing means a lot to him, so be a good dog and go pack his book bag and give him a snack.
Really, Mommy? I can go?

Only if you promise you'll be back before dawn.
I swear!

Monsters are helpful folk, and they very quickly began to make school supplies from odds and ends they found in the old house.

If you want a pencil, here's a piece of charcoal.
I should bring a present for the teacher.
Poop is always sure to please.
And Little Vampire flew out the window, very excited to go to school.
I'm not really sure about the poop.
You'll just have to wait and see what the other students do.
Besides, it's okay if you don't have a present on the first day. How would you know? You're new.
You're right.
As always.

It was a nice two-story school on the edge of town. There was a playground with swings, a sandbox, and an aviary full of doves.

In the hallway wooden hooks lined the wall at just the right height, so students could hang their coats.

But there were no coats.

The first classroom Little Vampire visited was empty, and so was the next one and the one after that.
I don't understand.

There are no students in this school.
Yes, there are.

Look, on each desk there's a notebook with a child's name on it.
I can't read very well.

Read me the names; maybe mine is one of them.
No.
I checked.

"Maybe students only go to school in broad daylight. And at night there's nobody here."

Yeah. I would say that must be it.

Little Vampire's mother had expected to see him come back at dawn, all excited about school, so she was worried when he came back early, hanging his head.
What happened, Phantomato?
Nobody's there at night. So he doesn't want to go anymore.
Didn't you give the poop out?
I don't like to see you like this. It makes me sad.
Yes, young man, especially since your problem is fixable.
Really, Captain? There's a way I could go to school?
Why not? If we all help out?

The next night, the ghosts agreed to meet at the school to make Little Vampire happy.

The Captain of the Dead, who was teaching class, had asked the ghosts to bring their own school supplies so they wouldn't write in any of the daytime students' notebooks.

Because ghosts shouldn't be noticed by mortals.

Well, I don't care. I'm going to write in the notebook.

The next day, in the same classroom, the schoolteacher asked her pupil: "Michael Duffin, did you do your homework?"

"Come on then, open your notebook," the schoolteacher said, "And read what you wrote." Michael opened his notebook and squirmed. Because, the truth is, he hadn't done his homework.

But there in his notebook, a miracle! His homework was done, and there were no mistakes!

Michael couldn't believe it.

Who could have done my homework for me?

That night, Michael left school without doing his homework.

"We'll see if the miracle happens again," he thought.

And on the next morning, he found his homework was done.
Cool!

And the next day, too.

Ever since he was little, Michael had been told many stories about the Good Lord: he parts the sea, he gives tablets with laws on them, he punishes Adam and Eve when they eat apples . . .

But nobody said anything about a Good Lord who comes into the school at night to do math homework.

Since Michael was afraid of coming to school in the middle of the night, he decided to leave a message in his notebook, addressed to his benefactor.

"Thanks for doing my homework. Who are you?"
Michael Duffin

The next day, there was an answer: "I am a vampire."

A vampire.

From that day on, Michael and Little Vampire left notes for each other.

I don't believe you.
First of all, vampires aren't real.

Oh, really? So who comes to your school in the middle of the night then?

I dunno. A burglar.

You think if I was a burglar I'd have nothing better to do than your algebra homework?

Maybe you're a burglar who loves math.

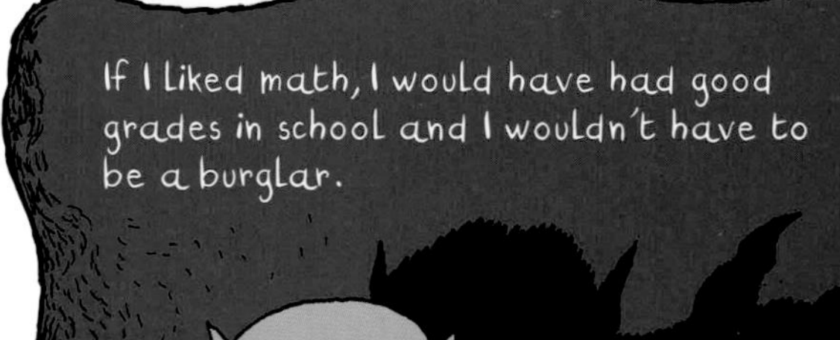

If I liked math, I would have had good grades in school and I wouldn't have to be a burglar.

Ha, so you **are** a burglar.

No! I'm a vampire. I'm a nice vampire and I'd like to have a friend and if you want to be my friend then I'll keep doing your homework.

What are you doing, Little Vampire?
Go away.
Sir, Little Vampire is writing in a student's notebook.
Is that true, Little Vampire?
No, no, no.
Show me that notebook.
The Captain looked at Little Vampire's note to Michael, and he became very grim.
Are you angry, Captain?
No. I don't usually get angry.
But what you've done is very serious.

You're endangering all of the monsters and ghosts. If people found out about us, they would tear down our old house and we would have to move again.
What can I do?
You're going to find this boy, this Michael, and you'll bring him to me. I must be sure he'll tell no one.
I don't know where he lives.
It's in the school records.
What do you think the Captain will do to him?
Kill him, of course.
But first he'll torture him! Ha! Ha! Ha!
Stop shaking— I'm only kidding!

Charles Street. Here it is.
Is that him?
RRR
ZZZ
No, they're old.
RRR
ZZZ
I hope we're not in the wrong house.
Hey.
Hmmrr?

WAAAA!!
Shut him up!
Shut him up!
Shhhh! There's no reason to be scared.
Mnfgmf...
Phantomato, make sure his mom and dad are still sleeping.
Sir, yes sir!
Your parents can't find out about me.
They're not my parents.
They're my grandparents.
I lost my parents.
Oh, really? Where did you put them?
Ha! Ha! You're funny. "Lost my parents" is an expression. It means they're dead.
Oh, yeah? Like me?
My parents, they're the living dead.
No, it's not the same.
Mine are the dead dead. That's why I'm an orphan.
If my parents were the living dead, I guess I'd be a vampire like you.
And what's it like, being an orphan?
Well, like me. You know, normal.
Okay, boss, the old ones are snoring like elephants.
This is Phantomato. He's my dog.
He's cool.

Wait...
Look, this is Alfonso, my fish. He's my friend.
I think he's ugly. A dog is better.
Don't mind him. He's just jealous.
He's not ugly, and he even knows me.
Really?
When you put your nose on the bowl, he comes.
Cool!
?
?
KABOOM!
Sorry.
You tried doing tricks to show you're better than the fish, didn't you?
Um, yeah.
Ha! Ha! Your dog is so cool!
You're not sleeping, Michael?
No, Gramps.
I...I found a dog.
He must have climbed up the gutter pipe and through the window. Can we keep him, please, Gramps?
We'll see tomorrow. Sleep now, little one.

Don't do this at home. If your dog isn't magical, you shouldn't climb on him.

Surprise!
Hi, monsters. Let me introduce. . . hey, where'd he go?
Michael! Michael! Come back. They're very nice.
Don't count on it.
Michael!
You're right to be hiding. They scare me, too.
They even stole a bone of mine last time.
AAAH!
Well, where were you?
I was peeing.
You shouldn't pee on tombstones, 'cause the skeletons will scream at you.
And they're very old, so they're pretty cranky.
It's because of their arthritis, my boy.
It's very damp where they live.
When you have moss in your joints, they creeeaak.

What are you doing, Captain?
I'm putting on a mask.
A human mask.
So I don't frighten the little boy too much.
Here, have a drink.
Is it blood?
No, no, it's chocolate.
Slurp
Monsters like chocolate too, my boy.
Good.
"Because I think those two look alike."
Heh! Heh! Heh!
Why are you laughing?
Ha! Ha! Ha!

The little boy is here, Captain.
Let him in.
I am the leader of the ghosts. Come closer.
Are you a pirate?
Yes. Long ago I was the captain of a Dutch ship.
When you were alive?
Yes.
My wife died the night of our wedding, by my own hand.
You killed her?
I thought she was unfaithful. It was a tragic mistake, and I was punished for it.
I was condemned to roam the seas on board a ghost ship, until I could find a woman who was willing to die for me.
Did you find her?
Yes, but I fell in love with her, and then I didn't want her to die.
But she killed herself anyway.
How did you know?
It's the story of the Flying Dutchman. My grandpa told it to me. The lady's name is Pandora, right?
Yes. That's Little Vampire's mom.
You can go home now.

You're not going to torture me?
How do you know I won't tell everyone that you live here?
I can see it in your eyes.
I was kinda hoping you'd make me swear on a skull or something.
You want to swear a pirate's oath? All right.
I swear to devote my life to protecting the dead and keeping their memory. And if I break my word, may a thousand curses befall me.
Now do the sign of the cross.
No. I can't do that.
It would give more strength to your oath.
But I'm Jewish, Captain.
The cross doesn't mean much to me.
Do the sign of the star, in that case.
We don't do that either.
And I don't believe much in God.
'Cause my parents are dead.
You're a bit young to believe in nothing.
Well, maybe he exists, Captain, but after what he did to me, I don't feel like I owe him anything.
You should think about all that some more. Sad times often open miraculous doorways.

Do you understand what he said?
No.
Do you have toys?
No.
Too bad. I have lots. My gramps buys them for me all the time.
I even have some waterproof ones, and they can go in the bathtub. You take baths, don't you?
No, I don't.
Ha! Ha! Ha! He never washes.
?
I don't get the joke.
Never mind.
Mommy! Mommy! Can we take a bath?
Yes, ma'am.
Why?
Vampires are naturally clean.
And monsters are so filthy there's no point cleaning them.
Just for fun, ma'am.
I don't get it. What's so fun about being in Liquid?
I don't see why not.
But I'm not even sure we have running water.
Huh! Huh!
We do have an old bathtub.
We'll find a way, Mrs. Pandora.

Is this the bathtub?
Yes.
Are you ready, monsters?
1, 2, 3, Lift!
The monsters ran off toward the swamp, carrying the bathtub with Little Vampire, Michael, and Phantomato.
Once there, it was easy to fill the tub with mud.
Make way! Make way!
Make way for the bath!
Ha! Sludge!
Ha! Ha!
shlomph! shlomph! shlomph!
The swamp creatures had never seen such a thing.
Even the grumpy old skeletons thought it was an unusual sight.
Ha! Ha! Bathtub Olympics!
Yay!
When the monsters put down the old tub on the oak table in the dining room, everyone came to see the bath.

Phantomato didn't like the idea of a bath, but he wasn't given much choice.
Come and swim.
Hey!
In the pool, blub blub blub blub...
Ha! Ha!
My, oh my!
What a mess you've made of the dining room!
This isn't funny. The Vampires' Ball is tomorrow night. Everything has to be spotless.

So everyone spent the rest of the night cleaning the dining room in the old house, so Mrs. Pandora wouldn't be upset. The monsters cleaned like crazy. One or two of them even licked the walls and said mud was tasty. But Michael cleaned with great care, because he was afraid he wouldn't be invited back to Little Vampire's home if the mess wasn't completely gone.

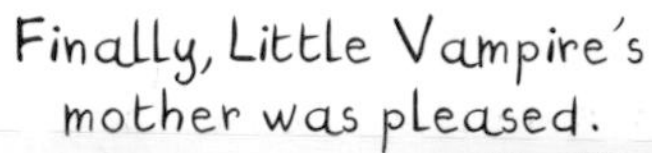

Finally, Little Vampire's mother was pleased.

She made tea, and Spanish cakes called montecados, which taste like shortbread, only better.

Krunch! Krunch!

But dawn was breaking.

In a flash, all the ghosts returned to their beds, their caves, and their tombs.

Good day.

Good day.

See you tomorrow. Sweet nightmares.

I don't have time to go back with you, Michael. Day is breaking.

Don't worry. I'll walk home.

I can fly you home if you want. I'm not afraid of daylight.
Great.

No, you'd better walk, Michael. I don't want anyone seeing a red dog roaming the streets in broad daylight.
You're right, Captain.

Goodbye, my friends, goodbye!
Michael walked through the sleeping village.
He climbed the wall of his home...
...and jumped into bed right before his grandmother came to wake him.
Get up, sweetie, it's time. I heard you found a dog.
Grandma, it disappeared.
What do you mean?

* Trust me, it's really yummy; you would have to have a grandma like mine to understand.

When it came time to hand in his homework, Michael felt confident because he knew Little Vampire had done it for him. But actually, no, he hadn't!
Little Vampire was with Michael all night, so he didn't have time to do it.
And Michael got an F, which taught him not to rely on other people to do his assignments for him.
From then on, Michael vowed he would always do his own homework . . .
. . . which would leave him more time to play with Little Vampire.
The END

"Little Vampire Does Kung Fu!"

...and that's how Peter Pan ended up in Kensington Gardens—but there's nothing to cry about, Michael.
Did my story upset you?
It's not about that, Gramps.
It's because of a kid at school—I want to kill him!
Don't say that!
But...
Sabrina and I were watching the bees...
and that jerk Jeffrey came and said they were flies.
shove!
!
So I told him no, they were bees because they were in the flowers—you see flies on poop, not in flowers.
That's true.
?
That made Sabrina laugh. But the jerk didn't like that, so he called me a loser and said I didn't have any parents.
I said, "That's a lie. I have parents, but they're dead." Then the kids all laughed at me and beat me up.
And I wasn't strong enough to defend myself, Gramps. They hit me in front of Sabrina, and that's really bad, and they even took my pants off in front of her! I wanted to be like you in the war and take a shotgun and kill every last one of them!
You mustn't think such things.

During the war I was a doctor before anything else. I healed people, even Germans.
That's not true! What about the Gestapo chief in Saint Jorioz, then?
Grandma told you that story? That was different: my life was at stake. You did the right thing by not fighting.
But Gramps, they humiliated me.
No. They're just idiots, and Sabrina knows that as well as you do. I never want you to fight, do you understand? They could have really hurt you.
And if it happens again, tell the teacher.
Yeah. Right. The teacher!
That Jeffrey, you wait for him at his house and then you bust up his face.
Then you take a knife and chop him into bits and send the pieces to his mom. That's the way to do it, right, guys?
Are you out of your mind?
What? That's not the way to do it?

I don't think that would be such a bad idea.
Yeah!
Michael... you're talking about killing a little boy!
Little or big, what's the difference? Once you're bad, you stay bad.
I think you're only saying that because you're angry.
And you guys, too! Come on, monsters. Get out of here, you're a bad influence on him.
Yeah, yeah, we're going.
He's making puppy-dog eyes; he wants to stay with us.
Only if he shuts up.
Woof!
C'mon, you can't be saying I should tattle to the teacher.
Nope. That's stupid.
Hop on.
Where are we going?
To see Rabbi Solomon.
A rabbi?
No, he's a kung fu master.

The kung fu master lives in your house?
Yes, in a painting.
Hello, Mrs. Pandora. You're as beautiful as the moon.
You're a very gallant young man, Michael.
I should've brought you some flowers.
My gramps always gives flowers to ladies.
Michael!
Yippee! In haunted houses you can go inside paintings.
Hi!
Hi!
Hi!
Hello!
Hi!
Hello!
Hi, guys!
Hello!
It's like that in other houses too, you know.
You should try it at your house. I'm sure it'll work.
Hi! Hi!
Ha! The one with the violin looks wimpier than the others!
He's the one we're going to see.
Yom Yom Vayom.
Shalom, boys. Shalom, dog.
Shalom, cat.
That's Solomon, the Catbalist.

Come on in. I have some good Baltic tea in my samovar from Samogotia. We'll add some slices of apple with honey. It'll be delicious.
That's a strange painting you live in.
It's called Let the Cat-Man Do.
I like it.
Pssst!
You got it all wrong. He's a rabbi. And rabbis don't know the first thing about kung fu. Look: he doesn't even have a weapon, and all he does is play the fiddle and munch on apples!!
You'll see. He knows plenty of things.
You have to help my friend, Solomon. Some kids are beating him up at school.
Is that so? In that case, we'll build a golem.
A what?
A giant dude. It'll go to school with you and protect you. It can even carry your book bag.
אמת
No.
That won't work. We're not allowed to bring giant dudes to school.

You have to teach him kung fu, Solomon.
Yes! Wushu kung fu, the boxing style of the Shaolin Temple monks.
You must read The Great Book of Kung Fu.
Oy vey iz mir! I don't remember where I put it.
It must be somewhere behind that door. Get it for me, Michael.
You guys coming?
No, no.
We're going to finish the apples.
Hm . . . it's sort of a garden.

What a strange place to forget a book!

There were thousands of monkeys in the garden.
They didn't look dangerous, but you never know.
Hoo!
Hoo!
Hoo!
Hoo!
Hoo!
Hoo!
Hoo! Hoo! Hoo!
Hoo!
Hoo!
Hey!
Hoo!
Hoo!
EEE!
EEE!
A
EE!
EE!
AAA!
Bing!
Bang!
Bang!
Bing!
Bing!
Bang!
Bop!
Bop!
Bang!
Bop!
Bing!
Bing!
Back off!
I want the kung fu book. Where is it?
With Lumpini the dragon...
All the way at the top of the temple.
Will you go get it for me?
Are you nuts? It's big-time dangerous up there. I'm not going.

It was an old Khmer-style temple.
But style wasn't Michael's concern.
All he could see was that the bricks were loose, wet, and mossy . . .
Oh, no.
And that all those old rocks were horribly slippery.
Ouch!
Ouch!
Ouch!
Bonk!
Bonk!
Bonk!
But Michael was so intent on learning to beat up Jeffrey that he didn't give up.
He observed the movements of the monkeys . . .
Hoo! Hoo!
Then he told himself that he was a monkey, too.
Hoo! Hoo!
That's the monkey technique.
?
EEee!
After many falls, and covered in bruises, cuts, bumps, and scrapes, Michael reached the top.
VICTORY!
Not quite, my young friend.

I am the Siamese dragon. They call me Lumpini.
Um... hi.
The book you are looking for is tied to my back. If you want it, you'll have to fight.
Here! Take the nunchaku and defend yourself.
Hey!
But...
Bop!
I don't know how to use this thing!
That, my friend, is your problem.
Bop!
Ha! Ha! Ha!
Lumpini! Lumpini!
Ouch!
Ouch!
Ouch!
Ouch!
!
Oh, noooooooo!
Don't give up!
Go back there!
Make him spit his teeth out!

Before going back up, Michael trained a bit with the nunchaku.
No need to do fancy stuff like Bruce Lee.
Hi-ya!
Just hold it firmly and whack hard with it.
?
Hi-ya! Hi-ya! Hi-ya!
Then the fearless Michael climbed to the top of the temple.
Hi-ya!
Even easier than the first time, he thought.
But then, he was really angry.
HI-YA!
And the real fight began.
It's nice of you to come back and see your friend the dragon.
And the monkeys started taking bets!
I'm going to help you go back down without getting tired. Ha! Ha!
Don't worry, I'll be gone soon...
Hoo!
Hoo! Hoo!
But not without my kung fu book!

The dragon acted as if he were drunk.
?
Hi-ya!
That's the noodle technique.
Bang
Bop
Bang
BOP
BOP

So you could never predict his movements.
Bonk!

Michael knew that to defeat the dragon, he'd have to act unpredictably too. He started rolling around on the floor.
?

Then he started singing silly songs to break his opponent's concentration.
?
Little Bunny ♫ Foo-Foo... ♫

And wham! He threw his weapon up in the air... the dragon looked up...
?

Big mistake!
wham!

The betting crowd went wild!
Wham! Wham!
Wham! Wham!
Wham!
Ow! Ouch! Ow!

And Michael won!
Bye, dragon! I'll bring your book back as soon as I've read it.
!

Do you think he'll be okay?
Sure. He's my pal.
Here's your book, Rabbi Solomon.
And next time try to be more careful about where you put your things.
Ha! Ha! Yes, that's the kung fu book all right.
Come here and help me read, would you? The print is too small for my eyes.
Let's see...
What?!
Is this a joke?
What's this supposed to mean?
Congratulations! If you have managed to steal this book from the dragon, you are very skilled at kung fu.
This book will teach you nothing more.
It means that after what you've been through tonight, you no longer have anything to fear from anyone at your school.
Really?
Of course.
The jerk shows up and you just rip his head off!

Michael, what's this walking around with no shirt?
Hi, Captain!
You're going to catch a cold!
A cold? No way, Captain! I'm a kung fu master.
Hm . . . Little Vampire, can you make sure that the kung fu master puts his pajama top back on at once?
Yes, Captain.
Hey! Hey! Hi, monsters!
Hi, friends!
Shhh! We're playing.
Come and see, boys.
This video game simulates fishing. It's wonderfully exciting.
Oh, yeah? Looks pretty boring to me!
Tonight Rabbi Solomon taught me how to fight. So tomorrow at school, Jeffrey's history.
Oh, Noooooooo.
Jeffrey won't be at school.
Why not?
Why not?
Because we went to his house and ate him.
Yes!
It didn't even wake up his mother.

Ha! Ha! They're so silly!
You didn't really think I'd buy that, did you?
It's...
It's a joke, right?
Well, no, my boy.
You said yourself that he had to be killed.
We ate him to make you happy.
Usually we prefer cakes to little boys.
I think they really did eat him, Michael.
Oh my gosh, they're crazy. If the teacher tells my Grandma, I'm gonna be in big trouble.
Listen, you absolutely have to put the boy back where you found him.
Yeah!
But we're telling you that we aaaaaaate him!
Well, spit him out! Because if the Captain of the Dead finds out about this, he'll make sure you get no chocolate for at least a week!
Oh, no!
That would be so cruel!
A whole week, gasp!

So the monsters spat up bits of Jeffrey onto the carpet.
Yup! I'd say it won't be easy gluing the pieces back together!
(Don't try this at home, especially if your mom has a nice carpet.)
Mommy, could you lend us your sewing machine?
Are you boys taking up sewing?
Yes, Mrs. Pandora.
Well, at least while you do that you won't be getting in trouble. Do you know how to use it?
Yes, Mrs. Pandora!
C'mon, get to it, guys!
Make sure you make small stitches, so no one can see.
Don't worry, I'm doing the ship-boy stitch.
What's that?
It's a pirate tradition. When they eat the ship's boy, they sew the skin back together to make pants.
Really? Cool!
tung
JEFRY PATURN
lyning
hemm

There!
Great!
You can't see the scars at all.
Hey, Claude, you've grown a sixth finger.
You're right. I have to clip them.
And now, to bring Jeffrey back to life, all we need to do is go see my daddy.
Why? Who's your dad?
Doctor Albrenstein.
So they went to wake up the ghost of Albert Einstein.
Doctor Albrenstein!
Who's calling?
But the scientist said that he wasn't Marguerite's father.
Dad!
?!!?
How cute.
And in any case that he did not know how to revive the dead, and that life, death, it was all relative anyway.
Dad...
I'm a bit absentminded, but if I had a son like you, I would remember it.
Maybe check the lost and found.
Albert, since you know about nuclear physics, can you come and change the battery on my radio?
And after that can you set the time on my VCR?
By the way, I forgot to tell you the names of the three monsters:
The one with three eyes is
Ophtamol
The one with the huge jaws is
Claude
And the kind of dumb one who likes poop is
Marguerite

Are you sure your dad is called Albrenstein?
Dunno. I'm not so sure.
It wouldn't be Frankenstein instead?
RIP
OLIN
No. That name doesn't ring a bell.
Just then, Albert Einstein came back.
Hey!
You again?
He said that although he didn't know how to revive corpses, he could build a time machine to go back in time, like in the movies.
Indeeeed! To go back in time, because time's all relative, you know...
Therefore all they'd have to do would be to go back in time up to when the monsters were about to eat Jeffrey and stop them from doing it.
And relatives ...
they can take up a lot of time.
Give us a break! A time machine! Everyone thought the doctor's imagination was running away with him.
But you can't sell that machine to the Army, you know. I've been down that road before.
He's lost his marbles big time.
Well, in any case, he can't be my dad, because he has a mustache.
He's bonkers!
So they waited politely for him to go back to bed.
And if you change your mind ...
Yeah, yeah, sure.
Geez!
Might as well face it, science wasn't going to be of any help in bringing back the dead. A solution had to be found, because they'd be in big trouble if that jerk Jeffrey wasn't brought back to life by morning.
I say, what we need is a magician.

Captain, do you know of a magician in the neighborhood?
Why?
We were just wondering, Captain.
You're not hiding something from me?
No, no.
I think you look like people who have gotten into some sort of mess. You really don't want to tell me anything?
No!
We want a magician.
Fast!
Later
I'm telling you, they must've gotten into trouble!
I know.
But if they don't want to talk about it, we must respect their wishes.
What magician did you send them to?
I sent them to the Felicity Tree. That way they'll have a choice.
The Felicity Tree was at the back of the garden, behind the mulberry trees, in a big Chinese pot. It was offered to Moses by Confucius, which explains its other ancient name, The Luminous and Legendary Tree of Chinese Hanukkah. It's a tree that dances softly and makes you feel good. It's the only place where magicians can meet without fighting. And fights between magicians are really serious.
Are we going in?
No. Magicians give me the willies.
You're right, my boy; let's head home.
Hey! Visitors!
I am Baroness Sabado, the Mercedes-Benz of walking corpses, Most Venerable Grandma of Toads. Welcome to tonight's open house.
Good evening.
Good evening.

They were about to have dinner. Having that many magicians in one place sure was convenient.

It was a delicious meal, and many incredible stories were told. They ate cakes from the other end of the world, some of which cracked and wriggled in their mouths as though they were full of small insects, but they were tasty...

Then, as the magicians gathered around the fireplace to blow smoke rings and sip Ork moonshine, the children were asked about the purpose of their visit.
We've come on behalf of the Captain of the Dead.
He was practicing with his sword and by mistake he chopped up a little boy from my class.
He's too busy to take care of these kinds of details himself, so he'd appreciate it if you could bring the boy back to life.
You see, we've already sewn him back together, so all you need to do is revive him...
His mom would be grateful 'cause she's already paid for school lunches all year.
He's crazy! They'll never believe him!
But thanks to the magic of the Ork moonshine, the magicians were prepared to believe anything, even Michael's lie.
No problem, pal!

Then each magician explained how he would go about reviving Jeffrey if Michael entrusted him with the job.
He died from a direct lack of air. We must redirect his digestive gasses toward his lungs.
Croak! I'd summon the powers of night.
Ha! I'd make him a zombie!
I'd send little elves to buy back his soul.
I'll hurt him so badly he'll wake up fast!
Why don't we fill him with flies?
That would make him look alive, at least.
Neither Michael, nor Little Vampire, nor Phantomato understood a thing the experts said. They didn't know whom to choose.
Well, young ones, which one of us do you want to call upon?
Well...
We don't really know.
Mmm...
It was at that point that Michael said the one thing that should never be said.
We want the best sorcerer among you.
Who's the best?
Very good choice, boy. I'm the best.
What did she say?
She said she's the best. Ha! Ha!
Hm.
Pardon me, dear Baroness, but I believe the lad said sorcerer and not sorceress. Therefore it appears to be me he was referring to.
You? Ha! Ha!
Why not that midget while you're at it?
Vat?
I think it's me they were insulting. For you, they'd've said "that retard" or "that savage."
Vat?

The Felicity Tree no longer danced. It was still.
I'll bet you can't even turn people into shrimp!
POUF!
As a matter of fact, you really couldn't call it the Felicity Tree anymore.
Who changed me into a shrimp?
!
Couldn't be me; some say I wouldn't know how.
Baroness, watch out, someone turned you into a green frog.
I am not a zafitch!
Perhaps a cabbage then?
What a mess!
Hm...
Ooops, sorry.
That's your normal face.
Come here, little shrimp...
I'm going to gobble you whole.
You'd've thought you were on a school playground...
Whoosh!
Bang!
Bash!
Pow!
Slam!
Kazam!
One where every kid has magical powers.
Suddenly cracks began to appear in the Felicity Tree.
!

Will you knock it off?
You ought to be ashamed of yourselves! Look at your tree. It's falling apart because of your nonsense.
?
?
?
?
Yeah, it's true. Do you even know what you're fighting about?
He said he was the bestest.
He won't let me do the reviving.
They called me a midget.
No, they meant me.
Really? Well, it's pathetic of you to fight about it.
That's true. I only fight over serious issues.
I mean, to get me into a fight, you'd have to pee around my fire hydrant or eat from my bowl, really serious stuff.
What?
I'll go pee around your hydrant and we'll see if you're so calm about it.
Hm.
What I wanted to say is, if you're so powerful, why don't you just revive him all together?
Together?!
Yes, that'd prove that you're truly wise.
And not some little babies who can only think of fighting.
Vat?!
No, it wasn't you they called a baby.
Zen who vaz it?
The dog, it was the dog.
What?
To cast a collective spell, we have to go out into the clearing.

In the clearing, in the middle of the stone circle...
We're here.
Move away. This is secret business.
If you watch, you'll be turned to stone.
Say, it's been a long time.
It kind of sounds like praying.
You can come now.
You see, we did a great job.
Yoohoo, Michael.
Miichaeeel!
Help!
What on earth have you done?
?
Miiichaeeeel!
He's alive; what're you complaining about?
But he's a giant!
That's your fault, buddy.
Huh?

You're the one who wanted us to work on him all together.
So what?
So what? C'mon, it's logical; if we resurrectionize him six times at once, it makes him six times more alive.
And six times more alive means six times bigger, obviously.
Yup.
You . . . you can't leave him like this.
Ha! You should make up your mind, kiddo.
We're out of here now.
Yup.
Oh no! Michael's going to get squashed. I have to go get the Captain of the Dead.
You're nuts! He'll kill us.
Do you have something to tell me, Little Vampire?
!
We'll tell you everything!
No need.
Get the little giant to drink these two vials. One will return him to normal size and the other will make him forget everything.
Hurry!
Thank you, Captain.

And the giant Jeffrey Jerk marched on.
He played with farms.
?
?
He played with cows.
BRRR
I've lost him, that goon.
Moo!
Moo!
Oh no! He's walking toward the villages!
Quick, Michael, climb onto Phantomato's back.
What the... whoa!
!
!
He's throwing cows at us!
Mooo.
Ready to dive, Phantomato?
Ready, pilot.
Roooar!
Eat that!
Grr...
And that!
Gulp!
POUF!

What am I doing here?
?
?
?
Hush...
You haven't seen or heard anything. I'm bringing you home.
Sleep well, boy.
ZZZ...
Are you sure everything will be okay?
Yes, you can go home.
Tomorrow Jeffrey'll be the same as ever.
Same as ever...
Ha! But I'm not the same as before.
I'm a master of...
kung fu! ...ZZZZ.

The next day, at school.
Hey man, you got it coming.
He's over there.
And he's flirting with Sabrina, too.
Get outta my way.
Hey, jerk!
Excuse me?
Watch this!
?
Monkey technique!
Noodle technique!
?
Up! Look at the book bag!
Whee!
?
Err...
POW!

And that's when Jeffrey got a book bag on his head.
Bonk!
Did he hurt you?
It's your fault, though. Why did you have to pick a fight with that bully?
Let me see your nose.
It's bleeding.
I only have my cloth handkerchief to clean it with. Do you mind if I clean you up?
It's okay. I'll do it.
I don't mind. I'll be your nurse.
Oh yeah?
Yeah, and I'll be a kung fu master, and you'll give me a kiss.
You want a book bag on your head too?
The End

"Little Vampire and the Canine Defenders Club"

As usual, the ghosts were haunting the old house.
BOOOOOO!
Among them was their friend, a little boy named Michael.
BOOO!
There was also a little vampire, called Little Vampire.
Hey guys!
Ha!
Ha! Ha!
Lastly, there was a ghost dog called Phantomato, because he was red like a tomato.
Hate to bother you, but some people have been knocking on the door for the last five minutes.
What people?
Those aren't people, they're dogs.
So?
That's no reason to not let 'em in.
What is it?
Let us in!
We're being chased!
Please!

This is a haunted house. It's not for dogs.
You'd get too scared.
It can't be worse than where we just came from.
I have to ask my mom.
Too late! They're barging in!
The dogs made their way into the house. They feared neither ghosts nor monsters.
Hurry!
Lock every entrance!
Calm down, ya mutts. We're not afraid of anyone.
If there are people who want to hurt you, we'll eat 'em, and that'll be that.
They're not listening to you, they're too anxious.
Poor fellas.
Outside.
BOOM! BOOM! BOOM!
Open up! That's an order!
All right! Don't know who that is, but I'm gonna make mashed potatoes out of him!
Certainly not, Marguerite.
No human can know we haunt this house.
We must hide ourselves and above all, make no noise.
Grrrr...

Everyone hid.

It's dead inside, Doctor.
You're joking—I see a light.

I think people are hiding in there.

And if they're hiding, they must not have a clear conscience.

BOOM! BOOM! BOOM!
Open this door!

Maybe I should go see.
What would you say to them?

I don't know, but it doesn't seem like I'm risking anything. I'm not a ghost.

And if they're bad guys, everybody jump out and cut 'em to pieces, OK?...

Who's there?
Police! Open up!

You don't look like the police.
Open up!

I'm home alone. My parents told me not to open the door for anyone.
Hmm... a kid.

Open up, little boy, and you'll get candy.
Not by the hair of my chinny chin chin!

That's it! Kick the door in!
Can't, boss. That's private property.

Hrrgh! Give me that shotgun!

BLAM!

My dogs are private property too.

So, you little devil, where are my dogs?
AAA!

Won't talk, eh?

Search every-thing.
Here, doggie!

Doggie doggie doggie.

L'il doggies!

No dice, boss.
This shack's totally empty.
Fine. Let's go then.
Whew!

I heard a "Whew!"
Wasn't us.

We didn't say "Whew!"
Don't take us back to the lab!

I – I'm an expensive purebred. I'm the Baron of Saint-Hubert! Sell me to an old lady-you'll make a lot more money!
Let's go.

Throw them in the truck.
Ahwoo
Ahwooo
Ahwooo

AHWOOO
VROOOM

You... you let them get away with it!

I swore never to kill more humans. I could not intervene.
I didn't swear nothin'.
Me neither. But we have to obey the Captain.
Yeah, yeah.... Fact is, once you saw it was just a bunch of dogs, you didn't care.
Watch your tongue, Phantomato.
Whatever...
If it'd been three children, or even three little pigs, you would've saved 'em, but who cares about dogs, right?
This makes me sick. I'm getting out of here.
Us too. Coming, Michael?
Goodbye!
What?
I should have risked the safety of all to save three dogs?
Stop looking so grave. What would you have me do? Go after the people from the laboratory and free the dogs, is that it?
No.

But I'm sure that's what Little Vampire's going to do.

I'd like someone to discreetly follow the children, just in case they need protection.

When I see what such people do to dogs, I don't dare imagine what they might do to vampires.

I'll go, Mrs. Pandora. I've got my scooter.

And if they touch a single hair on Little Vampire's head, I'll mangle 'em.
Little Vampire doesn't have much hair, Claude.

And I forbid you to use violence, do you hear? You must promise to be inconspicuous. Promise, Claude.

Yeah, yeah.

Can you see them?
Yeah.
The car's headed toward the river.

Ahwooo
Ahwooo
What's that sound?
Monsters?

No—I think they're the howls of mistreated dogs.

What about those, over there?
They look like giant molehills.
Boo! Boo! No moles in these mounds you'll find.
Boo! Boo! Just ghosts of the haunting kind.

Boo! Boo! Dogs here in their graves do lie!
Boo! Boo! Waiting for help to come by!
OK, but stop the Boo Booing, it's freaky.
Or just annoying.

We're the ghosts of dogs who've died here.
We'll know no rest until the lab gets shut down.

I'm Dracurla.
And I'm Mongrela.
A pleasure.
What do you mean, know no rest?

I mean that with all the dogs howling next door, we know no sleep.
Ahwooo
Ahwooo

WHIR WHIR
WHIR WHIR WHIR

Vroom vroom
Whoosh whoosh

HEY!

WHAM!

Whoa... what do you think you're doing?
We didn't want you going alone, Claude.

You're just slowing me down. Now I won't ever find the kids' tracks again.

My scooter's wheels are crooked.
Don't worry, c'mon.
We'll find them together.

Marguerite?
Yes?

Why are you pushing a wheelbarrow full of poop?
I don't know.

I thought it might come in handy.

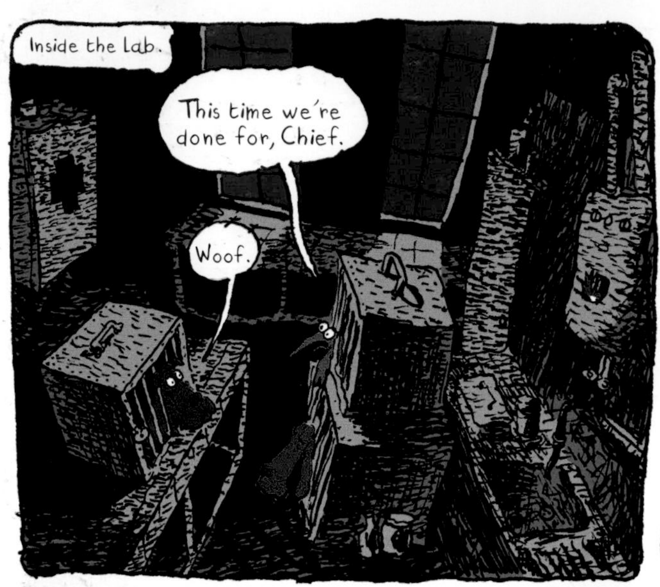
Inside the lab.
This time we're done for, Chief.
Woof.

They're going to make us eat lipstick and toothpaste until we keel over.

Well, maybe next time around we'll come back as something better than lab animals.
You believe in reincarnation, Chief?
Maybe so.

Maybe in a former life I was a beautiful woman who always slathered on the kind of lipstick put out by this lab.

And maybe I came back as a mongrel to see just what it's like to die of too much lipstick.

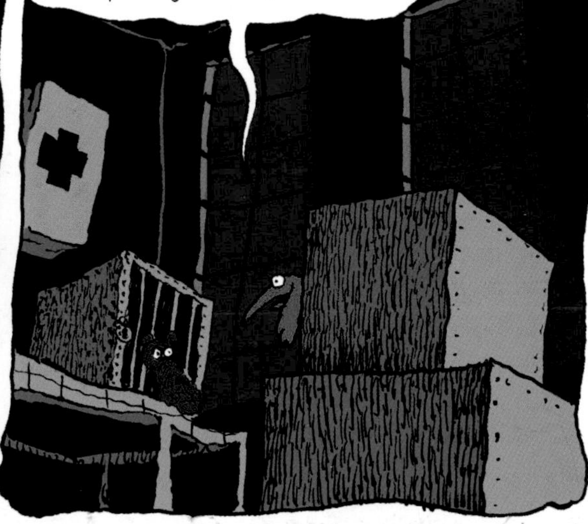
Tell us what it was like when you were a pretty woman, Chief.

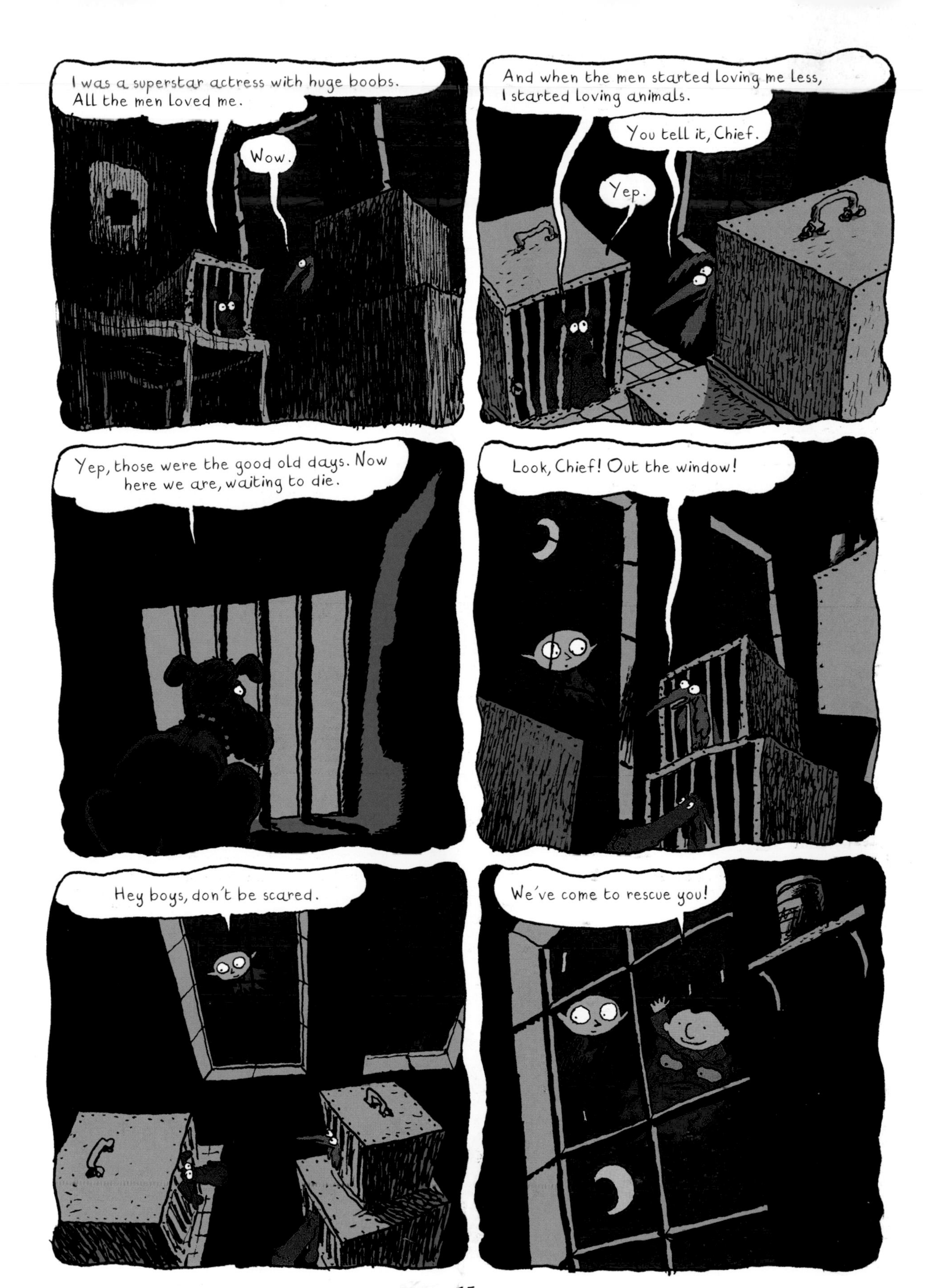

I was a superstar actress with huge boobs. All the men loved me.
Wow.
And when the men started loving me less, I started loving animals.
Yep.
You tell it, Chief.
Yep, those were the good old days. Now here we are, waiting to die.
Look, Chief! Out the window!
Hey boys, don't be scared.
We've come to rescue you!

Knock out a pane, Phantomato.
WHAM!

WHAM!
WHAM!

CRASH!

Padlocks!
Gotta find the keys.
Ouch!

What's all the ruckus?

Grrr...

A dog covered in lipstick!

Who can fly!

CHBOIIIINGBL
GRRRR

Put 'im in a cage. The boss'll be happy.

Find me a needle so we can knock him out.
OK...
GRRRR

Best to be careful.

Leave him alone!

KRAK!

My needle!

Don't worry, I'll give it back.

ZING!
WATCH IT!

BAM!

You're in for it now.

HEY!
A flying animal!
AAA!
I'll anesthetize it.
Then I'll dissect it to see what it looks like inside.
Heeellp, boss!
BLAM!
ZING!
Hmm! It should be asleep.

SECRET
BORATORY
ZZZ...
ZZZ...
ZZZ...
He's sleeping, boss.
But he's not coming down.
You free the dogs. That goon should have the keys.
OK!
I'll take care of Little Vampire.
Can't wake him. I better just get him out of here. Up and away!
ZZZ
Hey!
Incredible! A lipstick-covered dog!
Heeellp, boss!
I want that dog! Bring him back!
BLAM!
BLAM!
BLAM!
BLAM!
BLAM!
BLAM!
Learn to shoot, blockhead. Ha ha!
ZZ

ZZZZZ...
ZZZZZ...
ZZZZ...
Hey!

I'm gonna let go.

So let go – everybody's got problems.

AAA

SPLASH!

OH, NOOOO!

He broke my wheelbarrow!
I didn't do it on purpose.

I'm gonna destroy you!

No – the Captain said no violence.

Hooray! The dogs are out!
Michael!

Hey! Help me wake him up!

Wakey wakey, L'il buddy.
Eww... what a stench.

Sniff... sniff... I don't smell anything.
Marguerite!

My pal!

C'mon, let's go home.

What about us?
We don't have a home.
What are we gonna do?

It's OK for the Baron, he's a purebred.
But the rest of us are ugly mutts. No one wants to adopt us.
You don't want to adopt them, Michael?
No.

I don't think my grandma and grandpa would like three dogs.

Let's go to my house so we can think about it in peace.
Can we really all go to your house?
Not you three monsters.

And as soon as the sun rises, you guys leave too.

So the monsters went home, and the rest went over to Michael's.
I know!

Tomorrow during recess, I'll tell the kids at school there're dogs up for adoption!

There've gotta be three kids who'd be interested. Especially girls. Girls love pets.

The dogs grew hopeful again. They pictured themselves at home with nice new owners who groomed them and gave them big chewy bones to gnaw and soft pillows to sleep on.

Then they fell asleep, deeply moved.
ZZZ
ZZZ
ZZZ

And everyone slept.
ZZZ
ZZZ
ZZZ

The next morning when Grandma called, everyone was still there: the dogs, Little Vampire, and Phantomato.
Michael dear, breakfast is ready.
Yes, Grandma.

Yoohoo! You're going to be late for school. Do you want me to come upstairs and help you tie your shoes?
NO, Grandma, don't come up!

See Arthur, it seems our little one's learned to tie his shoes all by himself.
That's good, sweetie. He's a very smart boy.

BABADABOOM!
!
!

Can you tie my shoes, Grandma?

Grandma, Grandpa—you can't go in my room today.

It's too messy. I'll clean it tonight when I come home.

See you later, buddy.
Study hard.

What a sweet little boy.

I'm going to clean his room for him.

It'll be a nice surprise.

OH!

What's all this?

We're Michael's friends. We're not evil.
That's why he didn't want me in here. He had a friend sleep over and was afraid I'd scold him.

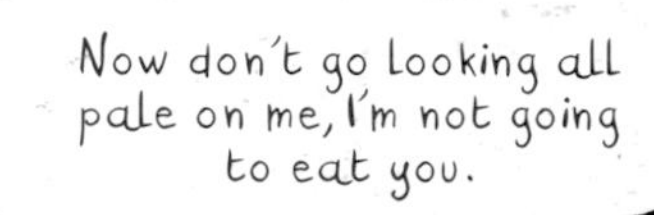
Now don't go looking all pale on me, I'm not going to eat you.

It doesn't bother me if Michael had you over. But no dogs on the bed—out!

This one's mine, ma'am. We found the others. They won't stay.

Shouldn't you be at school, little boy?
No, I'm sick.
That's true—you don't look well.

We'll go outside. You need some fresh air.
No, no—I can't have too much sun.

Then I'll make you a Hemzalleh with jam and some good coffee.
Do you have hot chocolate instead?

It seemed like that dog was talking!

No, it was me, ma'am. I'm hoarse.
You've come to us in quite a state. You're not very well-dressed, either. My husband should have a look at you. He's a very good doctor—you'll see.

ARTHUUUR!
DOCTOR'S OFFICE

Yes, sweetie.

One of Michael's friends is here, and he looks ill. You have to examine him.
TOR'S FFICE

He does look very pale. What's your name, son?
Little Vampire, sir.
Funny name. Is it French?

Take a deep breath.

Hmm... that's strange.

My stethoscope must not be working.

I can't find a heartbeat.

Hm. Even stranger...

I can't take your blood pressure. It's like you don't have blood.

I think we're going to have to take you to a specialist, son. Where are your parents?
I don't want to see a doctor, sir.

I'm not sick. I'm a real vampire.

Don't you believe me?

I feel quite well. It's just that I'm a vampire.

Do you believe me?

Of course I believe you.

Because it's the only explanation.

You're like a giant mosquito. You bite people to live.
Yes ... but not Michael, sir.

Michael's my best friend.

I have to go sleep now, sir. It's the middle of the day, and I'm tired.

Don't tell anyone what I am, OK, sir?

Otherwise, people could hurt me.

So, Arthur, what's wrong with the little one?
Nothing, sweetheart, just overworked.

I gave him something to help him sleep, and he's taking a nap now.

Really, Arthur, they push the children too hard, have you noticed? A little boy like that, and those giant book bags.

We'll have to see that boy's parents, Arthur.
adding machine with paper roll
complicated accounting
tax forms

I don't know what they're feeding him, but he looks like the living dead.

You're exaggerating as always, Cecile.
I'm exaggerating? Have you seen how scrawny he is?

That boy's skeletal. I'll go to the butcher's for some ground meat and make him some stuffed tomatoes. He needs some meat on his bones.

No garlic in the tomatoes, Cecile.
It's good with garlic.

Yes, but you know how children don't like garlic.

HERALD TRIBUNE

Still awake?
Yeah, I can't stop thinking.
You can call me Grandpa.

Yes, Grandpa.

CLAP!
CLAP!
CLAP!
CLAP!

You know, rumor has it that Michael's got a crush on your owner.
Maybe, Mr. Bibi, but I don't think she cares for him.

How about you, Mr. Baron? Doesn't look like it's going so well.
Bah.

Your owner's no good?
Well...

She's an adorable little girl. She plays the piano and I lie at her feet.

She reads me books, the classics: Balzac, Proust, Beethoven.

I like Beethoven a lot – it's the story of a big dog.

So what's the matter? Don't you eat well?
Yes. I've never been so well cared for.

But I think about my former mistress. She must miss me. She must think I'm dead.

Don't worry, Mr. Baron. We'll talk to Michael about it.

A few minutes later.
You're a good dog, Mr. Baron. I'll tell Little Vampire to take you to the old lady tonight.

It's just to reassure her, you know – to tell her I'm doing well.
Of course. Be ready tonight.

When night fell, Little Vampire and Phantomato went to fetch the Baron.

They brought him to the old lady's house, which wasn't easy, since he couldn't quite remember the way.
Y'know, there are dogs who can find their way back over hundreds of miles.
I'm sorry.
Don't worry, pal, even purebreds lose their way sometimes.

Wait – it's over there. I recognize it. The hosiery shop on the right.
HOSIERY

But the shop was closed.

Permanently.
CLOSED Owner Deceased

So the Baron went to the old lady's grave to pay his last respects.
AHWOOOO

Then he went home to his new owner.

And with her he was happy for the rest of his days.

Joann Sfar

Some fine offerings from **First Second** for young readers of graphic novels...

Kaput & Zösky
Lewis Trondheim
Town Boy
Lat
"Sweet, funny, and brilliantly drawn, Kampung Boy is one of the all-time great cartoon books."
–Matt Groening
Kampung Boy
Lat
Robot dreams
Varon
Tiny Tyrant
Lewis Trondheim & Fabrice Parme

New York & London

Published by First Second
First Second is an imprint of Roaring Brook Press,
a division of Holtzbrinck Publishing Holdings Limited Partnership
175 Fifth Avenue, New York, NY 10010

Distributed in Canada by H. B. Fenn and Company Ltd.
Distributed in the United Kingdom by Macmillan Children's Books, a division of Pan Macmillan.

Little Vampire Goes to School and *Little Vampire Does Kung Fu!* were first published in America by Simon & Schuster, Inc. in 2003.

Originally published in France in 1999 under the title *Petit Vampire va à l'école,* in 2000 under the title *Petit Vampire fait du Kung-Fu!,* in 2001 under the title *Petit Vampire et la société protectrice des chiens* by Guy Delcourt Productions, Paris.

Design by Danica Novgorodoff

Cataloging-in-Publication Data is on file at the Library of Congress.

ISBN: 978-1-59643-233-8

First Second books are available for special promotions and premiums.
For details, contact: Director of Special Markets, Holtzbrinck Publishers.

First American Edition May 2008
Printed in May 2009 in China by South China Printing Co. Ltd.,
Dongguan City, Guangdong Province

3 5 7 9 10 8 6 4